BOW DOWN IN JERICHO

Byron Herbert Reece, who with his first book, *Ballad of the Bones*, came into prominence not only as a powerful younger poet but more especially as a balladist, has done an even more outstanding job in this volume in which, as the title suggests, Biblical ballads play a large part.

The ballads are divided into two sections, Biblical and the usual type based on folklore to be found in the southeastern part of this country; these are followed by a generous group of lyrics and a section of typically fine Reece sonnets.

Few poets had the versatility of Reece; from ballads to lyrics to sonnets, each quite superb in originality and handling in its own field, is a wide range.

The lyrics link him with a long line of English-writing melodists: while deeply original, he had in common with them the love of land, the beauties of which only the countryman knows. Reece himself was a farmer and did not outgrow the wonder of that life.

This is a book, and a writer, to be greeted with pride and joy.

BYRON HERBERT REECE
(1917-1958)

Byron Herbert Reece was born and reared in a secluded mountain area of North Georgia near Blairsville. Before he entered elementary school, he read *Pilgrim's Progress* and much of the Bible, upon which many of his later ballads were based. As an adult, he was a lonely mountain man who was a modestly successful dirt farmer and a poet of surpassing genius. Reece had the ability to say new things in the old traditional forms, distinguished by their simplicity and accuracy. His poetry was mystical, lonely and often seemed preoccupied with death. Reece was perhaps the greatest balladeer of the Applachians. During his short life, he received two prestigious Guggenheim awards and lectured as Writer-in-Residence at UCLA, Emory University and Young Harris College. Reece died by his own hand on the campus of Young Harris College in early June 1958.

Other Cherokee titles by Byron Herbert Reece:

> *Ballad of the Bones & Other Poems*
> *Better a Dinner of Herbs*
> *The Hawk and the Sun*
> *The Season of Flesh*
> *A Song of Joy & Other Poems*

also: *Mountain Singer: The Life and the Legacy of Byron Herbert Reece* by Raymond A. Cook

BOW DOWN IN JERICHO

By Byron Herbert Reece

❈

Poetry

THE BALLAD OF THE BONES

BOW DOWN IN JERICHO

❈

Fiction

BETTER A DINNER OF HERBS

BYRON HERBERT REECE

BOW
DOWN
IN
JERICHO

 Cherokee Publishing Company
Atlanta, Georgia
1985

Library of Congress Cataloging-in-Publication Data

Reece, Byron Herbert, 1917-1958.
    Bow down in Jericho.

    I. Title.
PS3535.E245B6   1985   811'.54   85-21335
ISBN 0-87797-102-1 (alk. paper)

This book is printed on acid-free paper which conforms to the American
National Standard Z39.48-1984 *Permanence of Paper for Printed Library
Materials.* Paper that conforms to this standard's requirements for pH, alkaline
reserve and freedom from groundwood is anticipated to last several hundred
years without significant deterioration under normal library use and storage
conditions. ∞

Manufactured in the United States of America

ISBN: 0-87797-310-5

Published by arrangement with
E. P. Dutton, a division of New American Library

CHEROKEE PUBLISHING COMPANY
P.O. Box 1730, Marietta, GA 30061

For

ALL THOSE

whose friendship I claim

BALLADS

CONTENTS

LYRICS

CONTENTS

CONTENTS

SONNETS

BALLADS

I

BOW DOWN IN JERICHO

The Winning of Elijah's Mantle
II Kings, 2

I

And it came to pass when the Lord would take
Elijah up to heaven in a whirlwind's wake
Elijah said, "Elisha, now my time is near
And I must go to Bethel, pray you tarry here,
O I must go to Bethel, pray *you* tarry here."

But Elisha was a prophet and could read his mind
So he knew Elijah wanted but to leave him behind;
Was going over Jordan, was going there to die;
Said, "Must you go to Bethel? Then so must I.
O *must* you go to Bethel? Then so must I!"

And they two went down to Bethel,
And they two went down to Beth-eL.

And the sons of the prophets that were at Bethel
Came forth to Elisha with a thing to tell.
They came to Elisha and made their moan:
"Knowest thou tomorrow thy master will be gone?
Knowest thou tomorrow thy master will be gone?"

Were he then a prophet if he knew not so?
"Peace" said Elisha, "Yea, I know, I know."

"Now the Lord hath sent me unto Jericho,
Elisha," said Elijah, "and hence I go,
And the way is weary and there's much to fear
Of robbers, so I pray you, will you tarry here?
There's danger, so I pray you, won't you tarry here?"

But Elisha *was* a prophet and he answered, "No!"
And they two went together to Jericho,
They two went together down to Jericho.

And the sons of the prophets that were at that place
Sent forth a spokesman with a long, sad face.
He came to Elisha and he made his moan:
"Knowest thou tomorrow thy master will be gone?
Knowest thou *tomorrow* thy master will be gone?"

Now were he a prophet could he not foresee
What on the morrow was going to be?
So he said as soon as the man would cease,
"Yea, I know it, won't you hold your peace?
Yea, I *know* it, won't you hold your peace?"

Then Elijah said, "Tarry till I come again
For the Lord hath sent me over Jordan's plain."
But Elisha would follow till his wish was won
And they two went together to J-o-r-dan,
And they two went together down to *J-o-r-d-a-n*.

And the fifty sons of the prophets stood
And watched while they came to Jordan's flood.

O the waters of Jordan were wide and deep,
Too deep for wading, too wide to leap,
And Elisha wondered as the waves would toss
How, thought Elijah, they could get across,
How in safety they could get across.

But Elijah was a prophet and a man of God
Whose power was ever at his beck and nod.
He smote the waters and said, "Divide!"
And they crossed dry-footed to the other side,
O they crossed dry-footed to the other side.

And Elijah said when the flood was by,
The rolling waters of Jordan,
"What, Elisha, would you ask ere I
Am gone like the waters of Jordan?"

"If it please thee, Master," Elisha said,
"As you were coming from Ho-r-e-b,
Anoint Elisha, the Lord God said,
As you are going from Horeb.

"As I was driving the plodding kine
In the fields of Abelmeholah,
Thou cast about me the mantle of thine
In the fields of Abel-me-HO-lah.

"And then didst thou anoint my head,
In the fields of Abelmeholah,
To be God's prophet in thy stead
And I followed from A-BEL-me-ho-lah.

"And yet I have not got thy power,
Thou partest the waters of Jordan,
Ah, yet I have not got the power
To part the waters of Jordan!

"And this it is I would ask of thee,
This of thine would inherit
As thou art taken away from me:
The power of thy holy spirit."

"If thou shalt see me when I go,
Oh, thou hast asked me a hard thing,
Even as ye ask shall it be so
Though thou hast asked me a hard thing."

[15]

III

And the hour was come when the Lord would take
Elijah up to heaven in a whirlwind's wake.
And they two walking like son and sire
Were parted asunder by a chariot of fire,
The horsemen and chariot of Israel!

And Elisha *saw* how the wheels of flame
Were mounting up to heaven by the way they came,
And he shook with joy as they upward sped —
If thou shalt see me, had Elijah said,
If thou shalt *see* me had Elijah said. . . .

IV

Now Elisha rends his robe in twain,
Watch, ye prophets at Jericho,
With Elijah's mantle he comes again,
To Jordan, ye watchers of Jericho.

And he has smitten the raging flood,
Look, look ye watchers of Jericho,
Over Jordan he comes dry-shod,
Watch, ye prophets of Jericho.

He comes again into the town
Into the town of Jericho
And the prophets there they all bow down
Bow down bow down in Jericho!

REMEMBRANCE OF MOAB

II KINGS, 3

I

King Mesha had within his keep
Moab and a million sheep.

When he walked in the evening air
Among his swarthy shepherds there

As twilight brooded quiet and dim
A gnawing thought would nag at him:

*Moab's flocks and fleece that swell
The treasury of Israel*

*Might raise to me a throne of gold
Were Moab free of Ahab's hold!*

II

Before the campfires burning red
Mesha, king of Moab, said:

"Behold, a hundred thousand rams,
Also a hundred thousand lambs

"And fleece enough to snow the land
Each year we give to Ahab's hand.

"Is it because he tends our flocks
As wide they graze by rills and rocks,

"Or rouses from his bed of sleep
At lambing time, or stays the leap

"Of thieving wolf, Ahab should take
Our flocks' increase for Israel's sake?"

III

The shepherds roared in anger then,
Fired with the rage of simple men

They cried unto the king: "Rebel
Against Ahab of Israel!

"Send forth the word he shall not take
Tithe of our flocks for Israel's sake!"

And Mesha sat in his tent by night
And his heart was filled with a grave delight

To think that soon he should send and tell
Ahab: "My shepherd folk rebel.

"Send drovers forth no more to take
Fleece nor flock for Israel's sake."

Within his heart his stout words glowed
But not with a runner upon the road.

*The peaceful sheep on every side
Grazed white as foam on time's green tide.*

IV

Now Ahab still by day and night
Wrought evil to his heart's delight.

[18]

In the halls of his house of ivory
Gay were his evil queen and he,

And even the fierce red king of hell
Boasted no queen like Jezebel.

He, while the loud lutes swam in song,
Burst Naboth's grapes against his tongue;

And she with long, lascivious gaze
Looked down her lust-delighted days

That were but corridors that led
To languor in a wanton bed.

Though by her will in tent and town
Samaria to Baal bowed down

Her drowsing god did not foretell
The hour by the wall of Jezreel,

Nor how the queen should be at last
A dull gray dropping a dog had cast!

v

It came to pass that Ahab sate
With Judah's king before his gate

And said to his prophets standing by:
"Look to thy gods and prophesy."

The tongues of the lying prophets said:
"Get thee to Ramoth-gilead.

"O get thee to this place and stand;
God gives Syria into thy hand."

And Ahab, turning another way,
Cried: "What does the son of Imlah say?"

Micaiah said unto the king:
"I see concerning thee no good thing,

"But a flying arrow that wounds thee deep
And Israel scattered abroad like sheep."

And Ahab he was angry then,
And the lying prophets spoke again:

"O go thou up to deeds of valor
The while Micaiah acquires a pallor

"And eats, to pay him for his treason,
Affliction's bread in Amon's prison!"

VI

With Judah's king Ahab went forth
Against the Syrians to the north;

And early in the battle's din
He stood disguised amongst his men.

An arrow from a random string
Went flying forth and smote the king.

The blood from the mortal wound he got
Dripped down to flood his chariot,

And the dogs, as the prophet said they would,
Set their red tongues to Ahab's blood.

From king to king the kingdoms pass
While time's green tides run through the grass.

VII

The news went forth on every side
How Ahab, King of Israel, died.

Mesha heard in his tent of skin,
And he said to his simple shepherd men:

"Before our feet are set upon
The border our battle is halfway won,

"For hear you not how the runners tell
That Ahab is dead in Israel!"

Then Mesha numbered his fighting men
Man by man for the battle when

The news came to Jehoram's ear
That Moab thrust the revolting spear,

That Moab lifted the sword to be
Lord of its borders and wholly free.

VIII

For Jehoram in Ahab's stead
Ruled in the land of Israel,
He sent to Judah's king and said:
"The shepherd Moabites rebel,
The insolent shepherds of Moab;

"And I have numbered my fighting men,
Every warrior in Israel;
Wilt *thou* go up to battle, then,
Against these shepherds who rebel,
The insolent shepherds of Moab?"

Jehosophat of Judah said:
"If thou art ready let us then
Go take the king of Moab's head!"
And they went up, and all their men,
Through the wilderness of Edom.

IX

O these two kings and all their press
Went up to war, and Edom's king,
For seven days. The wilderness
Was bare and dry, a withered thing;
And there was no water in Edom.

And Israel's king he said: "Alas,
That we three kings the Lord should call
To wither here like common grass,
Or under Moab's swords to fall,
Israel and Judah and Edom.

"The cattle lacking drink will die,
And we no less, and all the host;
And our unburied bones shall lie
To witness how our cause was lost
In the wilderness of Edom."

"Let us have hope," said Judah's king,
"And fall not in a battle yet
Unbattled. Let us send and bring
A prophet of the Lord; yea, let

Us three unto Elisha go
With gifts such as our stores afford
And make inquiry of the Lord."

x

The three kings to Elisha came
And bowed them down on bended knee.
And he of the prophetic fame
Said: "What have I to do with thee,
O what have I to do with thee?

"Arise again and get thee hence,
God hates thy brash impenitence.

"Assault Him not with cry and wail;
O get thee to thy prophet Baal.

"God looketh not toward thee at all;
He numbereth each sparrow's fall.

"He marks their goings in the sky,
He hears each little fledgling cry,

"But when you call in doubt and fear
Thy words He will not deign to hear.

"When from the heart His laws are dropped
Toward plea and prayer His ears are stopped."

But, all bowed down on bended knee,
The three kings to Elisha still
Made moan and supplication shrill:
"For word from God we come to thee.

[23]

"For we three kings the Lord would call
To wither here like common grass,
Or under Moab's swords to fall,
And we three kings are kings, alas!"

Elisha said to Judah's king:
"Were thou not throned on Judah's throne
I had not answered thee a thing
But get thee gone, but get thee gone.

"But bring to me a minstrel gay
And let him harp his harp upon
And then if God has aught to say
I listen, and His will be done."

XI

With nimble stroke and plucking sharp
The harper harped upon his harp.

He looked upon the waiting kings
And harped a song of royal things.

He looked upon Elisha there
And harped about a robe of hair.

He saw the rabbit bound away
And harped his burrow in the clay.

He saw the flocks feed on the hill
And harped their bleating high and shrill.

He saw a bird on rising wing
And harped the song the linnets sing.

And higher still he raised his eye
And harped a cloud calmed in the sky.

And yet again he looked beyond
And harped the shining of the sun.

Into the noon arc gazing straight
He harped a chord at heaven's gate.

At heaven's gate a chord harped he
And for the gate it was a key.

The strings went spying through God's brain
And to the prophet came again

Where he sat bowed beneath the sun
Too tranced with God to look upon.

XII

Elisha raised his holy head
To speak them what the harp had said.

He said unto the waiting kings:
"The waters of a hundred springs

"Were not enough thy drouth to slake,
Yet in this valley ditches make.

"Nor rain shall come nor wind shall blow
Yet water from the dry sands flow

"And man and beast whose tongues are burst
Lean down to drink and quench their thirst,

"And marvel at a wonder wrought.
Yet this is but a thing of naught

"To Him who in time's morning spanned
The reach of chaos with His hand,

"The olden order brought to pass,
And turned time's green tides through the grass.

"Now He who set all things to rights
Gives into your hands the Moabites."

XIII

Now when the break of day was nigh
The thirsting heard the water sigh.

Who listened for no better sound
Heard floods of water coming down.

Who thought that they should drink no more
Awoke to hear the water roar.

To such a sound as sleepers deem
The dire invention of a dream,

A phantom water come to slake
An actual thirst, did they awake.

As one they rose, each man and beast,
Kings, carls and cattle, great and least,

Knelt down together by the moats
While water cooled their thirsting throats,

Then rose to sing: *Praise be to God*
Who gives the thirsting water.

XIV

The Moabites in martial order
Came and stood upon the border.

They came and glistened in the sun,
All who could put armor on,

And looking eastward saw the flood
Of sun-touched water red as blood

And thought their armor on in vain.
"The kings," they said, "are surely slain!"

Each cried out to each: "O brother,
The kings have smitten one another,

"Have spared us of the battle's toil;
Now, therefore, Moab, to the spoil!"

XV

So they came down, and all was well
Till they came to the camp of Israel.

Then did the hiding Israelites
Come forth and smite the Moabites.

And the Moabites to their own country
Went back as fast as they could flee.

And the Israelites like a turning wind
With fury chased them close behind.

And so they smote, and had no pity,
Every fenced and choice walled city.

And it was given unto them
To fell the good trees trunk and limb.

And every fertile piece of land
Received a stone from each man's hand.

And furiously they fought, and well,
And the battle went to Israel.

XVI

But Moab lacking heart to meet
The bitter issue of defeat

Would try with offering if the price
Of victory be sacrifice

And bound and burned upon the wall
Edom's heir, grown tan and tall.

The flames ate of his flesh and blood
Until the stench rose up to God.

"Be sure," God said, "I shall remember
Him that hath perished in the ember;

"And thou, for this iniquity,
Moab, I shall remember thee

"Until, debased beneath the dust,
The root shall pierce thee with its thrust!"

Mesha and his shepherds sleep
Beneath the grass cropped by the sheep.

Their ghosts rise on the winds, and pass
As time's green tides run through the grass.

THE LARKS AT THE MEETING

OF DAVID AND JONATHAN

I

David the shepherd boy
From Bethlehem sped
To the host of Israel
With a few loaves of bread,

His harp at his shoulder,
Psalms in his throat,
And cheese from the milkings
Of an old she-goat.

He spoke with his brothers,
His song rang blithe,
And he took a stone and flung it
And killed Goliath!

As soon as he was come
From that fray with victory
King Saul said to Abner:
"Whose son is *he?*

"Go bid him forth."
And so David went
From his brothers to the king.
When he came to Saul's tent

Puffed as a toad
With what he had done,
His heart skipped a beat
When he looked on Jonathan.

O were I the brother
Of such an one, he said,
And stared while his vision
Of the king and glory fled.

And a lark in a thicket
And a lark in a cloud
Sang both together
As those two bowed.

So the son of Jesse
And Jonathan
Found each other
In the morning of the sun.

Jonathan
Was the son of the King,
And David was a shepherd
With a harp and a sling,

But fair as a lily
And lithe was he,
And the color of roses
And ivory.

David was a harper
And his harping was fair
Till he looked on the king's son
Through a mist of cloudy hair.

His harp had then
A voice of its own
And what it played then
Was *Jonathan*.

David was a psalmist
With a golden tongue,
But he looked on the king's son
And he forgot his song.

He looked on the king's son
And he forgot to sing,
Then his heart was strung
With a single throbbing string

And the tune of love
That string played on
Was *Jonathan, Jonathan
Jonathan*.

O, thought David
As he gazed his fill
When I watched the sheep
High on some lonely hill

Would that we together
Had woke and slept;
O that we together
The watch might have kept,

His hand on my shoulder
Perilous and kind,
And the little lambs playing
And baa-ing on the wind!

And the lark sang to David
From low in his mind,
And the lark sang to David
From a thicket twined.

II

David was a shepherd
Lithesome and tall
But Jonathan
Was the son of Saul.

A hero of battles,
The doughty Jonathan
Was the hope of the people
And king Saul's son.

Now what should the son
Of the king of Israel
Have in his heart
A shepherd lad to tell?

"As I would clothe me, even,
Against the rain and sun
Here is my robe, David,
For thee to put on.

("For surely I shall carry
Till my days are no more
The image of David
At my heart's still core.)

[32]

"As I would arm me, even,
To warrior for my Lord
Here is my blade, David,
Buckle on my sword.

("For surely I shall carry
Till the two of us part
In death the image
Of David in my heart.)

"As I would smite, even
Farther than the spear,
Here is my bow, David,
For thee to bear.

("For surely who shall rive it
When it beats no more
Shall find David's image
At my heart's still core.)

"As I love thee, even,
I strip me of my girdle,
The royal symbol, David,
To bind about thy middle,
    David,
To bind about thy middle!"

And the lark sang to Jonathan
Lovely and loud,
The lark sang to Jonathan,
The lark in the cloud.

THE CROWS AT THE PARTING
OF DAVID AND JONATHAN

Above the stone of Ezel
Querulous and high
Through the broken morning
Did the caw-crows cry.

They alone had witnessed,
And the eye of the sun,
The banishment of David
From the sight of Jonathan.

Jonathan, shooting
While his lad stood apart,
Loosed three arrows,
(From his bow to his heart,)

Loosed three arrows
Eastward at the sun,
And when his lad sought them
He cried: "They fell beyond!

("Past all finding
The arrows speed apart
That signal David's going
And the death of my heart.

"Past all knowing
The arrows have flown
That turn him to the wilderness
And my heart to stone.")

When the little lad, laden
With the bow had gone,
David came from hiding
By the great black stone.

And they two in silence
While the shadows at tether
Followed forth the sun
Sat bleeding together.

As each to each aching
Their slashed wrists bled
Jonathan, caressing
The palm of David, said:

"As I was dreaming, David,
    Dreaming of thee,
    Fair and kind, David,
    You came to me.

"Against my heart, David,
    I dreamed you leaned to rest,
    But I might not embrace thee
    And honor in my breast.

"Your fevered fingers, David,
    Burned mine like a brand,
    But I might not caress thee
    And honor in my hand.

"Your lips were sweeter, David,
    Than dew where honey drips,
    But I might never kiss thee
    And honor on my lips, David,
    And honor on my lips.

"But now thou art banished
    From the house of Saul
    And I shall not encounter
    Thee daily in his hall,

"Nor press with thee to battle,
  Nor listen to thy lyre,
  I lean to thee to kindle
  My heart to fire.

"Since henceforth thou art banished
  Forever from my sight,
  (See the sun falling
  Westward into night,)

"And I no more may wait thee
  Whatever place I stand,
  I take thy own to handsel
  Love's fury in my hand.

"And yet, now thou art banished
  By Saul from Israel —
  Until the time fulfilling
  The dreams of Samuel

"When the seeming endless
  Way thou must set upon,
  Proud path that in the turning
  Shall lead to Israel's throne,

"Brings thee again to Gibeah,
  I lean to kiss thy chaste
  Lips brushed with salt of sorrow
  And death's dear honey taste.

"Now may the Lord forever
  Keep watch between us two."
  So Jonathan and David
  Said adieu.

When David's form retreating
Was little on the plain
And Jonathan had turned him
Homeward once again,

Above the stone of Ezel,
Querulous and high
In the broken evening
The crows began to cry:

"Jonathan, Jonathan
The son of Saul
Turns about from Ezel
To seek the end of all.

"Turns his face from Ezel,
Does the son of the king,
Looking toward Gilboa
As if it were the ring

"Set with the seal
And signet of his race,
Turns about from Ezel
His death-devoted face,

"Turns about from Ezel,
From David, all alone
And looks toward Gilboa
As if it were his throne.

"Jonathan, Jonathan
The fair son of Saul
Hastens forth to Bethshan
To hang upon the wall,

"Saying: *Did David
But trample with his feet
My bare bones blanching
My death were sweet;*

"*And his hot hands about them
Shall be close as my flesh
As weeping he buries them
In the sepulchre of Kish!*"

THE REMEMBRANCE OF JONATHAN

"Jonathan hath yet a son"

II SAMUEL 9, 3

Now in the halls of Israel
When he was king and lord
David had one
Who feasted at his board.

High among the sages,
First among the strong
In a place of honor
He sat before the throng.

Among the carls so splendid
And captains of the host
To drink the wine of splendor
Sat the crippled ghost.

And nought the king demanded
Of mild Mephibosheth
But rouse him up of mornings
And draw his breath

And by the look
That he had on
Remind the king
Of Jonathan,
    Jonathan,
        Jonathan,
            Jonathan.

MARY

As Mary did in Nazareth bide
She was a maiden then;
She had no thought to be a bride
Of angel or of man.

As Mary was in Galilee
Upon her bed of sleep
She did not dream a wife to be
A house and hall to keep.

As Mary did in Nazareth card
And spin the wool for cloth
She chancèd to the good regard
Of man and angel both.

For Joseph lived in Galilee
Who was of David's house;
Kindly on the maid looked he
And craved her for his spouse.

As Mary did in Nazareth bide
She heard an angel sing:
"Thou art the chosen for his bride
Who is in heaven king.

"Thou shalt conceive in summertime
  And in the winter drear
  When all the world is white with rime
  A strong son thou shalt bear."

  And Mary laughed in Galilee
  As only maiden can:
"Now tell me how this thing shall be
  Since I know not a man!"

  The angel spoke for God his host,
  In Nazareth spoke he:
"The power of the Holy Ghost
  Shall overshadow thee.

"The sun shall shine in Galilee
  And shine upon a clod,
  And that which shall be born of thee
  He is the Son of God."

  In Nazareth dwelt Mary mild,
  She carded and she spun;
  On Christmas Day she bore the child
  Of God, His Holy Son.

THE SHEPHERDS IN SEARCH
OF THE LAMB OF GOD

"Hush, is that a lamb I hear
  Crying in the cold?"
"A lamb? No shepherd's fire is near
  And neither pen nor fold."

"If not a lamb what is it cries
  Unhousen in the waste?"
"Perhaps it is the wind that sighs,
  Now let us all make haste."
    "Aye, aye, aye."

"Look, the stars have left the sky
  And nestle in the boughs."
"Nay, but Bethlehem is nigh
  And many a lighted house."
"Haste, and let us turn within
  And after Christus call."
"Nay, he is not housed with men
  But cradled in a stall."
    "Aye, aye, aye."

"Hush, I hear the lowing kine
  Tread gently on the straw."
"Haste, remember thou the sign
  Given by him we saw!"
"See, the cattle stand and nod
  Close by the Lady's feet."
"Look, the little Lamb of God
  Cradled where oxen eat!
    "Oh! Oh! Oh!"

THE ADORATION

If I but had a little dress,
A little dress of the flax so fair
I'd take it from my clothespress
And give it to Him to wear,
    To wear,
And give it to Him to wear.

If I but had a little girdle
A girdle stained with the purple dye,
Or green as grass or green as myrtle
About His waist to tie,
　　To tie,
About His waist to tie!

If I but had a little coat,
A coat to fit a no-year-old,
I'd button it close about His throat
To cover Him from the cold,
　　The cold,
To cover Him from the cold.

If I but had a little shoe,
A little shoe as might be found
I'd lace it on with a sheepskin thew
To keep His foot from the ground,
　　The ground,
To keep His foot from the ground.

If my heart were a shining coin,
A silver coin or a coin of gold
Out of my side I'd it purloin
And give it to Him to hold,
　　To hold,
And give it to Him to hold.

If my heart were a house also,
A house also with room to spare
I never would suffer my Lord to go
Homeless, but house Him there,
　　O there,
Homeless, but house Him there!

CHRIST JESUS HAD THREE GIFTS
FROM MEN

Christ Jesus had three gifts from men,
All in the stable where He lay,
From Wise Men seeking grace to win
At Bethlehem on Christmas Day.

The first gift was a gift of gold,
All in the stable where He lay,
To buy Him garments against the cold
At Bethlehem on Christmas Day.

"The Christ Child has a lovely face,"
All in the stable where He lay,
Said one, and he was clothed with grace
At Bethlehem on Christmas Day.

The next gift was an odor sweet,
All in the stable where He lay,
Him to anoint from head to feet
At Bethlehem on Christmas Day.

"The Christ Child He is fair of limb,"
All in the stable where He lay,
Said one, and grace was given him
At Bethlehem on Christmas Day.

The next gift was a rare perfume,
All in the stable where He lay,
That Wise Man dreamed of Joseph's tomb
At Bethlehem on Christmas Day.

Then, 'Wise Men, grace abide with thee,'
All in the stable where He lay,
'Redemption shall my one gift be
At Bethlehem on Christmas Day,
On Christmas Day in the morning.'

THE PILGRIM AND THE FIR TREE

The fir tree went to Bethlehem
OLD LEGEND

As I came down to Bethlehem
To see the Christ Child good
The foremost pilgrim that I met
Was the fir tree from the wood.

His boughs shook softly on the wind
As stoutly on he strode,
And kindliness, as in my mind,
In all his boughs abode.

"O tell me, sturdy Pilgrim,
Far from your land of snow,
What did you see in Bethlehem
Where lately you did go?"

"I saw the Magi from the East
Come riding one by one;
The Virgin biding with the beasts
I saw, I saw her Son

"Close cradled in His mother's arms
And cuddled to her cheek
As if one sought to do Him harm,
And she began to speak.

"She said, Thy trunk is big about,
  Shades in thy branches brood,
  Forsooth, but thou art dark and stout
  Enough to make a rood!

"I felt her dark foreboding sweep
  Like winter through my boughs
  There where the Christ Child lay asleep
  In the shadow of Herod's house."

THE COCK IT CREW IN HEROD'S HALL

The cock it crew in Herod's hall
  And startled host and guest;
  The cock rose in the dish to call
  Christus natus est!

The cock crew twice in Herod's hall
  As loudly as at morn;
  The cock rose in the dish to call
  Jesus Christ is born!

The cock crew thrice in Herod's hall
  That roasted in the pan;
  And Herod shook to hear it call:
"Thou art a cursed man.

"The first by Him who is the Christ,
  The next by God His Host,
  Father and Son, and that is twice,
  Next by the Holy Ghost.

"The two are higher than the sun
  And deeper than the sea,
  The last it is the third of One,
  The Holy Trinity.

"The first shall through thy fingers pass,
  The next shall smite thy hand;
  The third shall cry in heaven, alas,
  When thou in Judgment stand:

"I know thee not who knew not me!
  And crying from within
  Thy heart shall bear against thee
  Witness more than men."

JOHN: A NEW TESTAMENT BALLAD

I

"O who is that with raven tress
  And fire-face, crying in the wilderness?"

"It's John."

"Who is it shouts so loud and rude,
  Who speaks so sharp to the multitude?"

"John."

"His words seem dark to mate his hair,
  What does he cry on the desert air,
  What cries John?"

"He cries unto the people there:
  The way of Christ the Lord prepare,
  Does John."

"What else are those who come advised?"

"Repent, repent and be baptized,
  Says John.

"Though water has no power to save,
  And I baptize in Jordan's wave,

"Another cometh after me,
  With heaven's fire baptizes *He!*
  Says John, John, John."

II

"The people cry from every hand:
  What must we do to wear His brand,
  John?"

"And what does he reply to them?"

"Love and repentance pleases Him,
  Says John.

"And: He that has more coats than one
  Let him give to him with none,
  Says John.

"Let each when he sits down to eat
  Share with him who has no meat,
  Says John."

"And these are faithful sayings all,
  But the Centurians to him call,
  And what does he to the soldiers say?"

"Be content with Caesar's pay,
  Says John."

"Why does he say such a foolish thing?"

"To save his neck from Caesar's string,
  Does John, John, John."

III

"Oh who is this that comes afar,
  In shadow shining like a star?"

"That is Christ come to the tide
  Swift as a bridegroom to his bride."

"And is it He from the water led,
  The dove of heaven on His head?"

"Yes, that is Christ comes to the Shore
  All laved in light from heaven's door."

"But why has He blessed John with His touch?"

"Because his words have pleased Him much,
  Have John's, John's, John's."

IV

"Now that the Lord's from Jordan gone
  To east and west to claim His own,
  Has not the prophet's task been done?"

"Yes; yet he has a starker one,
  Has John, John, John."

V

"O who is that with cape and crown
  That close beside his queen sits down?"

"That's Herod sits upon a throne
  Beside a queen that's not his own,

"Full in the sight of the people, he
  The monarch of iniquity."

"And whose is the head on a plate of gold
  Herod has given the girl to hold?"

"John's."

"Why, then, did Herod cut it off?"

"To stop the sounding of his cough,
  John's cough when Herod would go to be
  With his brother's wife unwidowed."

"And does he hear the sound no more?"

"He hears it now as he heard before,
  As he shall hear it till he lies
  With Caesar's coins to close his eyes,
  The cough of John the Baptist."

"Well, Herod long at rest has been,
  Lying the grave's stark width within.

"The good thing out of Nazareth
  Has rendered up His mortal breath,

"And John the Baptist looked of late
  With dead eyes from Salome's plate;

"All in time are drowned and dim —
  Have we not heard the last of them?"

"Not so, for Herod lives again
  The million lives of sinful men,

"And Christ the Lord on Easter morn
  Held death's dominion up to scorn;

"And though betimes his rest is deep
  John may not always silence keep.

"He quiet lies and does not cry
  As long as men put evil by,

"Keeps silence till men bow to sin
  And then he wakes and cries again,
  Does John, John, John!"

BALLAD OF THE TRAVELERS

I

Three travelers at break of day
Walked on a leary lane
That led by Christ's town on the way
Ere leading forth again.

The first that fell upon their sight
As they approached the town
Were three tall crosses laved in light
Toward the sun's going down.

As they stood gazing from afar
There came a stranger, dressed
In gold-embroidered robes as are
The rich men from the West.

The one amongst them first to meet
That stranger drew his sword,
For he was one who found that sweet
Which taken coins afford.

But as he raised his sword to smite
That stranger where he stood
The triple crosses leapt in light
To his blond blade drawn for blood.

That lion let the lamb pass
To shelter in the dell,
And with the sound of breaking glass
The first cross shook and fell.

It fell upon the left hand
Cleft from its broken stob,
And never more that cross did stand
For Tom no more did rob.

II

As they three walked the winding way
Which to the walls drew nigh
They met a lovely lady gay
With warm and asking eye.

The one amongst them first to meet
That lady played a fife
In serenade, he finding sweet
A maid but not a wife.

[51]

But as she gaily nearer drew
The place where he did stand
The image of twin crosses flew
To the slim fife in his hand.

That serpent bade that bird pass
In safety from his spell,
And with a sound of breaking glass
The next cross shook and fell.

It fell upon the right hand
And rotted down to dust,
And never more that cross did stand
For Dirk no more did lust.

III

As they three walked a littered lane
That thrid the entrance gate
A blind man tapping down the main
Soon stood aside to wait

For alms with withered hand outstretched
That leprosy had burned;
As he foremost to meet him retched
And from his pleading turned

Cold heart and arctic eyes aside
And made as if to pass
A shadow fell across his pride,
Medallioned bright in brass.

Then he that turned away with pride
Turned back again with alms,
And, glassed in gloss, the shadow died
From the coins pursed in his palms;

And like a thunder-stricken tree
Or tower razed by a spell
The third cross from its base leant free
And thundered as it fell.

It lay upon the middle hand
Till rot its atoms ate,
And never more that cross did stand
For Hart no more did hate.

And "Rest ye, Christ, from Calvary,
And rest ye, thief and loun,"
And, "Rest ye, for we travelers three
Have won your crosses down!"

BALLADS

II

THE RIDDLES

When summer hung upon the bough
And field and wood were green
O'Brady and his body-groom
Were riding fast between.

"What news, what news," O'Brady said,
"What news bring you of home
That in the three long years befell
Since first I crossed the foam?"

"Good news, good news," the servant said,
"Good news of farm and field;
Each fall of three you were away
Full heavy was the yield.

"The mow is bursting with the hay,
The crib sags with the corn;
The wool would blanket all the poor
That from the sheep was shorn.

"The lean swine fatten on the grain,
The cattle on the grass;
And all your will that you made known
Servants have brought to pass."

"Good news you tell of field and farm,
Good news I'm glad to hear;
Now tell me of my house and hall
And of my Lady dear,

"For I had rather hear her well
And happy and at ease
Than have the yield of all the farms
Far-fenced in by the seas.

[57]

"And I had rather hear her fair
    And sweet, as at farewells,
    Than be the master of the hall
    Wherein our sovereign dwells.

"For I had rather hear her true
    And faithful as my bride
    Than have a deed to all the world
    That is so rich and wide."

"My mistress she is well I ween
    And fairer than the sun;
    My mistress takes her ease enough
    While maids on errands run."

"And is she true?" O'Brady said,
"And is she true to me?
    And is she true, my bonny groom,
    As she did swear to be?"

"O she is true, and so I swear,
    As ever lady was,
    And she is true enough, master,
    Though wonders come to pass."

"What wonders do you speak of now,
    Of witch or conjurer?
    And what have wonders one and all
    To do with me and her?"

"The greatest wonders of the world
    The wildest wonders known; —
    The corn springs in my master's fields
    Though not a seed was sown.

"The ewes grew great, or Easter fell,
  When nights were long and cold
  And lambed by ones and twos and threes
  Though all the rams were sold.

"The mare that draws my master's plow
  And makes the furrows run
  Foaled the first quarter of the year
  Though stallion there was none.

"The doe that haunts my master's woods
  And pastures in the rye
  Dropped then a little spotted fawn
  Though not a buck was nigh.

"My master's Lady bore a son,
  The fairest ever seen,
  When he had twice-twelve-months been gone
  And seas surged them between."

"Great wonders, these!" O'Brady said
  And prodded with the spur
  And silent they two rode the miles
  That lay 'twixt him and her.

And when he entered at his door
  The child was out of sight,
  And his fair Lady greeted him
  With words that showed delight.

Said, "Come and rest you by my side,"
  Said, "Come and feast with me,
  For it is three long, weary years
  Since first you crossed the sea!"

He said, "I'll sit down by your side
As soon as I am shown
The corn that springs up in the field
Though not a seed was sown."

Said, "I will feast beside my love
When I come from the fold
To see the lambs the ewes have dropped
Though all the rams were sold."

Said, "I will drink my Lady's health
In wine when I have run
To see the colt the mare has foaled
Though stallion there was none."

Said, "I will kiss my Lady's lips
So pretty-primped to sigh
When I have found the fair fawn dropped
Though not a buck was nigh.

"And I will lie beside my love
Nor turn till break of day
When I have kissed the son I sired
Three thousand miles away!"

The two they passed into the fields,
The corn grew shoulder-high,
And though they digged about the roots
Seeds there were none to spy.

The two they left the field behind
And passed into the fold;
The young lambs gamboled in the sun
Though all the rams were sold.

The two they passed into the stall,
There shadowed from the sun
The colt was suckling at its dam
Though stallion there was none.

The two they passed into the woods
And looked both low and high,
And there they found the spotted fawn
Though not a buck was nigh.

The two they passed into the hall
And entered at a door
And there they found the fair young son
Playing upon the floor.

O'Brady sat down by her side
As soon as he was shown
The corn that sprang up in the field
Though not a seed was sown.

O'Brady feasted with his love
When they came from the fold
To see the lambs the ewes had dropped
Though all the rams were sold.

O'Brady drank his Lady's health
In Wine when they had run
From looking on the young colt foaled
Though stallion there was none.

O'Brady kissed his Lady's lips
So pretty-primped to sigh
When they had found the fair fawn dropped
Though not a buck was nigh.

But when he saw the child at play
His heart was turned to stone
And from the door he came away
And left the child alone.

"I'll read your riddles now," he said,
"I'll riddle them a-right;
  And when I have your riddles read
  I'll lie with you all night.

"The corn was planted grain by grain
  Nor sown abroad like rye —
  And I have read you riddles one,
  Now tell me if I lie!

"The rams went to the market place —
  I read you riddles two,
  And there were butchered in their strength
  But each had known a ewe.

"The stallion champed above the mare,
  I read you riddles three,
  And then was auctioned at the Fair,
  But big with foal was she.

"The buck had traffic with the doe,
  I read you riddles four,
  Before an arrow found his heart
  And he was seen no more.

"And now but one remains to read
  Before we take our rest:
  My groom is father of the child
  That suckled at your breast!"

They two slept in a mouldy bed
And dreamless went to dust;
His sword that slew them both was red
With blood, and then with rust.

THE FABLE IN THE BLOOD

With Mary my love I went down to the Fair;
So winsome was she in her leaf-green dress
That many a youth who looked on her there
Sighed for her loveliness.

My Mary whose hair was the color of wheat
Ripened to gold in the fields of June,
Walked with a ripple as if her feet
Moved to an inward tune.

And she would be dancing, but I would not
For deep in the stream of my dark blood ran
A fable of hell that my fathers had got
From the faith of the Puritan.

And so we were parted by my blood's stream
That widened between us as ever it flowed;
And soon she went from me, as fades a dream
Dreamed on a lone-went road.

And a lad who saw her go singly there
Asked her to dance to the sound of the strings;
His teeth were like pearls and black was his hair
As the raucous raven's wings.

And she with a smile that was bitter to see
Accepted his arm and went dancing away;
And afterwards what was the music to me
Or dreary or gay?

Though I tried to be merry with many a lass
All through the day I was searching my mind:
Where shall I hide me till they shall pass
The homeward throng behind?

By Weatherton's water? By Coulson's wood?
By hedge or haystack? By stone or tree? —
By dark Beaton River whose boiling flood
Runs raging to the sea!

Or ever my lean shadow leant from the west
Softly I stole, and my black hate beside,
And swift and furtive as thieves we pressed
To Beaton River wide.

We hid us from sight in the grain grown tall,
Tensely we crouched in the windy green rye;
For the welcome sound of their first footfall
Waited my hate and I.

As soon as the dusk was beginning to sift
Gray as dove feathers from east to west,
Happily homeward began to drift
The holiday throng, to rest.

And two who came passing paused often to kiss,
And last by the waters of Beaton's dark flow, —
Loud did the cat of my black hate hiss
As I leaped upon them so.

My knife blade baffled his bone-girt breast
And quickly as ever his heart it pierced
Deep to the heft in her warm flesh pressed
At hers it quenched its thirst.

With a roiling of ripples ran Beaton's dark flood,
Quickly, Oh quickly I plunged them in —
Now where shall I shelter me, O my God,
Against the damning din,

The sound of their crying that hammers the air,
The roaring forever of Beaton's dark flood,
The rendering louder than I can bear
Of the fable that flows in my blood, my blood. . . .

TO THE DANCE GO THEY

"O Daughter, go put on your gloves and gown,
  The stars are out over Tilden Town,
  And lassies and lads to the dance haste down.

"Why do you sit in the gloom alone
  As sad as a dove whose mate has flown?
  Why are you not to the dancing gone?"

"Mother, the night is as black as soot
  And I am too weary to lace my boot;
  To the dance go they who are light of foot."

"Daughter, why sit here from day to day
  As still as a stone and as pale as whey
  While youth and the summer steal fast away?"

"Mother, ask not why I sit so still,
  Sad and staring beside the sill —
  Who asks no asking hears nought of ill."

"O Daughter, say why has your true-love strayed
  Away from your side to another maid?
  Once to you only his court he paid."

"Mother, why meddle to pare my pain? —
  The dreariest drought comes after the rain
  And the bee to the robbed flower never again."

PRETTY POLLY

"Pretty Polly goes dressed in red;
  Her laughing lips have bestown no favor
  But I'd stand all day on the top of my head
  For a taste of their hurtsome flavor.

"*A true-love never goes gay, goes gay,*
  A scarlet dress is the badge of folly;
  The gown of a true-love's drab, some say,
  But red suits pretty Polly.

"When pretty Polly is seen abroad
  Be sure there's always a beau to squire her
  Around the stones in the rocky road
  And lift her over the mire.

"For he cares not for his Sunday suit
  By half so much as a miser's measure,
  Nor takes a thought if he scuffs his boot
  For pretty Polly's pleasure.

"Son, the counsel I give to you
Is, shun the lass in a skirt of folly.
But who'd give a hang for a love that's true
If he could win pretty Polly?

"What lad has eyes for their hodden gray
Or a glance to spare for the dowdy lasses
Or half an ear for a word they say
When, laughing, Polly passes?

"I courted Polly in shade and shine,
Her hands met mine with their touch of fire
But she would not set me a table to dine
On the food of my heart's desire.

"The girl I took to my board and bed
Is kind of heart, and she's plump and jolly;
She has caused me no grief since ever we wed,
But she is not pretty Polly.

"And pretty Polly will never be mine,—
To love her still is the height of folly
But as long as the sun has the strength to shine
I'll long for pretty Polly.

"I'll long for pretty Polly."

I'LL DO AS MUCH FOR MY TRUE-LOVE

I'll do as much for my true-love
As any a young man may;
I'll sit and mourn all at her grave
For a twelvemonth and a day.[*]

[*] The Unquiet Grave, Child Ballad 78.

Yet as he sat the grave beside
A day but barely one
He said, "It's hard to sit and grieve
While my hawk wheels toward the sun."

But still he sat the grave beside
Where his true-love was lain;
O still he sat the grave beside
And his tears fell down like rain.

Now as he sat the grave beside
And wept upon the ground
He said, "It's hard to weep two days
And the fox before the hound."

But still he sat the grave beside
As he had sworn to do;
O still he sat the grave beside
And his tears fell down like dew.

As he sat by the grave's side
Nor wiped his eyes at all
He said, "It's hard to weep three days
While my horse waits in the stall."

Still he sat by the grave-side
Of her whom he had kissed;
O still he sat the grave beside
And his tears fell down like mist

The fourth day by the grave's side
The tears dried on his cheek.
He said, "I mind another maid
With whom I used to speak.

"It's hard to weep four long, long days
  Beside a clay-cold form;
  It's hard to love a clay-cold maid
  While living maids are warm."

His first love in her clay-cold bower
He's left to take her rest;
He's plucked to him a second flower
To wear against his breast.

BALLAD OF THE BRIDE AND GROOM

I

Every young man in the countryside
Knew that Tom had taken a bride;

And all the young girls for miles around
Knew that Teenie a groom had found,

And all who yearned for a holiday
Came to the house of the groom to stay,

Gay with pleasure and the malted grain,
Till the sun should send them forth again

To the plow and the churn and the broom and the scythe.
The bridal pair and their guests were blithe

As only they can be who know
How swiftly the hours of pleasure go,

How swiftly burn the candles that light
A space for joy in the hurrying night.

II

O the young guests danced to fiddles and sang;
And the blood in their throbbing temples rang

Because they knew the bridal pair
Were lying together above the stair

Drowned deep as death in ecstacy,
As they had every right to be

Being bridegroom and being bride
No other had ever lain beside.

Before the sun had yet risen up
The young guests, brave from the whisky cup,

The young on the bridal morning said:
"O Tom and Teenie lie long abed!"

And they cried for the bridal pair to rise
And rub the sleep from their drowsy eyes.

Then laughter among the young guests leapt
Because they knew that none had slept

In the bridal house but the very old
In whose slack veins the blood ran cold.

III

But the bridal pair said not a word.
They lay in silence as if they had heard

Nothing of all their young guests said.
In loving silence they lay abed.

And the sun came up and the gay young men
Might stay no longer to look again

On the fair bride blushing from her head to her toes
As if she were looked on without her clothes,

(She knowing well how she should find
Her fair self naked within the mind

Of each if she could but look within).
At dawn to the stares of the gay young men

She did not come blushing, and the young men went
Afield to work, and well content.

IV

Nightlong the girls in kitchen and corner
Sat, each with the bloom of love upon her.

And now and then would the young girls sing
A song about some happy thing

And blush rose-colored to look and find
What the tall young men had most in mind,

Seeing clearly, and not surprised,
Desire pooled in their naked eyes.

When the sun in the east was a finger high
They each rose up with a happy sigh.

Thinking how in the night just gone
One like them for the first had known

What it was to yield for good
The last, last, last of her maidenhood,

They rose to right the place, and sang
A song about some happy thing,

Then each the way she first had come
Set out by hedge or highway, home.

v

And so the morning to noon arrived.
The two looked out on the day that thrived

As they had hopes their love would do,
The love that was burning between the two

As warm as the midday sun, as bright
As the full-formed moon against the night.

The two came into the parlor where
Sat the old who had learned to bear

Such trades of life as when four sit sad
In order that two might lie down glad.

The old ones' faces and slack hands spoke
Of years gone over, gone up like smoke

Into a sky no whit more blue
Because its color is added to

By more and more of the selfsame tint.
They thought of life, how all lives spent

Since first in Eden the thing of sod
Rose stumbling up with the breath of God

Are utterly gone to nothingness,
Making no life more for the lives less

Except in the province of the mind.
Long since to such knowledge were the old resigned.

They knew that love would not be lost
Between the two, who knew love's cost

After the audit of many a year.
"Still, love in lasting will cost them dear,"

Thought the old who knew desire
Grown more of water and less of fire.

"She with her halo of hair like gold
And lips like berries will at length grow old

"And he remember — her fresh youth lost —
The early image, and to her cost.

"And he, for all he is strong and fair,
Will stoop and the gray come into his hair,

"And she remember his strength of thigh
And back and biceps, and turn to sigh."

Thought the old who were soon to wed
With death: "The two that have lain abed

"In young love locked all morning long
Will lie for longer amid the throng

"Of silent brides and grooms who meet
Loveless in death's cold bridal suite."

VI

But as for the two who were wed but a night
Life loomed endless — and that was right.

BALLAD OF THE LOST SHOES

The folks that live by Burney's Run
Heard first the doleful news
Of how Squire Basker Tarkington
Lost a fine pair of shoes.

He paid a pretty price for them
At Granny Fearny's store,
But they were leathery and trim
And very well they wore.

Old Basker Tarkington, folks say,
Is square and straight as steel
But never was a man to pay
For dancing toe and heel.

The shoes sat primly by the fire
And trod the path to milk,
But never danced a measure nor
Peeped forth from folds of silk.

At nine the shoes were by the bed,
At dawn were on again.
Their prints were round the milking shed
In sun or snow or rain.

They pointed straight along the trace
From doorstep to the well,
And marked the road that leads to grace
At the white church in the dell.

And once a week they trudged the mile
To store and home again,
Not once companioned past the stile
Nor through the lonesome lane

Till late one summer afternoon
They wandered from the Squire,
And travelers were seeing soon,
Plain printed in the mire

Without a sign of turning back,
Four footprints side by side,
A little track and a large track
As if of groom and bride.

Now people tell how hard it was
On Tarkington to lose
His docile leather pumps, alas,
His meek and mindful shoes.

He sought them everywhere, they say,
And sought them all in vain
— His daughter wore them once away
And never home again!

THE BEETLE IN THE WOOD

"Because the beetle that lives in the wood
  Is *knock-knock-knocking* aloud, I fear
  Some ill is afoot in the neighborhood.
  Death-knock of the beetle I hear.

"I wonder who it is going to die?
  Girl's or granny's the fearful fate?
  Nobody here in the house but I,
  Nobody here but my lone . . . but wait . . .

"Last night betwixt two lids of sleep,
  And all in the drowsing house grown still,
  I heard the sound of something acreep
  Over the window sill,

"And what was that sound as I swept the soot
  From the whitewashed hearth I had scoured with care,
  That sound as of a fumbling foot
  Stepping now here, now there?

"When night like a black cat comes to sneak
  Up the stairs, I think too much . . .
  What was that brushing against my cheek
  With a stealthy moth-wing touch!

"No rest tonight though my best geese gave
  Their breasts to pluck for my pillow of down.
  It's quiet, quiet almost as the grave . . .
  Now I hear the screech owl's sound,

"And all my bones are atingle with dread,
  And midnight passes, and one o'clock,
  And the beetle still in the wood of the bed
  Is *knock-knock-knocking* . . .
                          is *knock-knock-knock* . . ."

A BALLAD OF JAMES EDWARD OGLETHORPE

*A Member of Parliament named James Edward Oglethorpe had
a friend who was thrown into a debtor's prison where he contracted small-pox and died. Oglethorpe was so moved by this
occurance . . . he determined to do something for the better class
prisoner.* — R. P. Brooks, History of Georgia

It's seventeen hundred and thirty-two
And George the Second sits on his throne,
And little else has he to do.
(And the men in the debtors' prison moan.)

James Oglethorpe walks by the Thames;
He watches the tide run out and in,
And the Sunday air is filled with hymns
(And the prayers of the debt-imprisoned men).

James Oglethorpe walks on and on;
The face of his friend who died in jail
Is faint in the air like the cloud-veiled sun.
(Shall the prayers of the prisoners prevail?)

The face of his merry friend who died
In a debtor's cell of the raging pox
Is faint and sad and solemn-eyed.
He sings a song and his voice mocks:

"When George the Second sits down to dine,
(Oh, who can brook a king's desire?)
The jailbirds make him music fine,
The jailbirds carol from every shire.

"For Law, the fowler, has spread his nets
And birds must lose their use of wing;
Oh, all poor-plumaged birds he gets
Must sit in a cage to please a king!

"Must sit in a cage by night and day . . .
Oh, who will take a horn and blow
Till the high walls shake and fall away?
(A ram's horn conquered Jericho!)"

James Oglethorpe sits with the King,
Long and long have the two conferred,
In his heart he means a noble thing.
(Shall the prayers of the prisoners be heard?)

"Release these prisoner poor," pleads he,
"To pay their debts with silks and wine
From the fertile fields by the Southern Sea.
(A ram's horn grows from his design!)

"Between the Altamaha and
Savannah to the Mississip
There lies a rich and fruitful land."
(Oh, the ram's horn lies against the lip!)

He pleads and pleads; the King agrees:
"I grant the land that lies between
The Carolinas and the seas.
(Oh, the prison walls begin to lean.)

"Under the Royal Standard take
And plant the land and gather all
Its harvests for our sovereign sake."
(The horn has conquered the prison wall!)

James Oglethorpe walks light of heart
Over the streets of London Town;
And soon will the good ship *Anne* depart.
(Praise God, for the prison walls are down!)

James Oglethorpe steps to the shore,
The Georgia wind blows through his hair;
Out of the ships the jailbirds pour.
(O praised be God for an answered prayer!)

THE FAREWELL

With mad March straining
At bough and eave
I woke to a morning
Of taking leave.

By such a dress
As day had on
I knew the press
Of sleep had gone,

And yet, enchanted
Or yet a-dream,
Where my father's planted
I followed the team.

By sorrow foretortured,
I know not how,
In the upland orchard
I followed the plow

Where wide and narrow
The wind in glee
And the falling furrow
Followed me.

When noon was nighing
To the upland high
A youth came crying,
"Good-by, good-by!"

The friend I had
When we were young,
His voice sad
And low as song

Hushed half to silence,
Came and stood
By the orchard fence
In the white dogwood

And said: "Farewell,
For I today
Am gone to dwell
A world away.

"Bloody and broken
Beneath far skies,
War's wasted token,
My body lies.

"Each day you prayed
The missile meant
For my heart be stayed
Or strayed or spent.

"The fatal missile
Ignored your will.
An empty vessel
Lies under the hill;

"The stuff that filled it,
  My living blood,
  When the bullet spilled it
  Flowed into the mud.

"Your care was tender
  But given in vain,
  I have come to render
  It back again

"That you may spend it
  Still to thrive
  Because you send it
  To man alive."

  His spirit wavered
  From out my trance —
  His dust has favored
  The soil of France —

  From the orchard's edge
  His spirit fled,
  And the maple hedge
  Leafed all in red.

  Apple and peach
  Put forth their bud
  And the globes of each
  Were stained with blood.

THE HEART AND THE HAND

Fitz-James stood by his castle wall
And from the tree by his right hand stood
The fruit of day before its fall
Hang ripe and red as blood.

Fitz-James lifted his strong right hand
And caught the sun in his fingers four,
And it burned in his clutch like a flaming brand
And lighted up his door.

It lighted up his lintel low,
It lighted his door that was low and wide,
And through to the dark I saw her go,
His fair and five-month bride.

I saw his bride to the darkness go
And the door was shut, and Fitz-James stood
With the laggard sun in his right hand O
Where it burned as bright as blood.

And Fitz-James stretched his left hand out,
And I beheld a marvelous thing:
Something his fingers were caged about,
And it began to sing.

"What is that cries, that cries with woe,
 What is that cries in your strong left hand?
 What is that cries in its strange cage O
 I almost understand?"

"It's nor the lark that sings so sad,
 It's nor the thrush that sings so wild,
 It's nor the mockingbird gone mad
 And it is nor a child.

"It's nor the wind the leaf gives tongue,
  Nor the brook the smooth stones orchestrate;
  It is nor a thing that has ever sung
  Or ever will, soon or late,

"Save here in my hand as I pluck its strings,
  Save here as I pluck its strings apart,
  Save here as I crush it because it sings;
  It sings in my hand — your heart!"

And I heard, and it was my heart that sang
In the cage of his hand like a lost thing.
It cried like a bird lost out of its nest;
It cried for its home in my empty breast.

And I said to him who held my heart:
"How did you rifle my ribs apart
  To steal my heart from out of my breast
  Like a bitty bird from its hidden nest?"

And he lifted my heart in his hand and cried:
"I did not thieve it from out of your side.
  I looked to the winds, and it was there,
  I plucked it forth like a bird from the air.

"I did not thieve from your side, I vow,
  I plucked it with apples that hang on a bough.
  I did not enter your side to loot,
  I digged it from under the rose's root.

"It was your heart, not I, to blame;
  I did not take it but free it came,
  As even a sparrow to pick a crumb
  Held for its bill 'twixt my finger and thumb.

"As even a cat in my warmth to bask,
  As even a dog a bone to ask;
  As even a pony to nuzzle my sweets,
  As even a beggar to taste of my meats.

"Came as a stranger with me to dine,
  Came for a visit and was not mine;
  Came to be petted and fled from reach;
  Begged as a sinner will God beseech.

"Came as a spider a web to spin,
  Came as a fly and was caught therein.
  Was even a stick for the lame to grasp —
  I stooped and took it, and held an asp.

"Once as a leaf on a scented breeze
  It flew; I caught it — it stang like bees.
  Came like a needle to knit the torn,
  I stooped and took it, and held a thorn.

"Came as a golden, heady draught,
  I sipped it slowly — it turned me daft.
  Last as a potion the sick find good
  I drank its poison into my blood!"

  Fitz-James stood by his castle still
  And my heart it cried in his strong left hand
  And the sun at the height of his window-sill
  In his right burned like a brand.

  And I said: "Throw down, throw down the sun
  And give my heart back into my side
  And turn to the face in the window wan,
  O go you in to your bride."

And Fitz-James opened his fingers four
And the sun from his opened fingers fell,
But my heart he crushed in his hand the more
And it cried like a thing in hell.

My heart it cried, it cried in woe,
It cried in fear, it cried in rage;
It cried in the clutch of his left hand O
For the safety of its cage.

And Fitz-James said: "When the trees to war
March forth, or the grass in the rolling tide
Of the seas take root, I will restore
Your heart to your empty side!"

Then I said: "If he will not let you go
Turn in his hand a keen blade O."
And my heart heard me and obeyed
And turned in his hand a two-edged blade.

"If he will not free you as I desire
Turn in his hand a coal of fire."
And fire there burned in his left hand's cup,
And the smell of his burning flesh rose up.

"If he will not free you for thrust nor burn
A nail and a nail for each hand turn,
And still for the finished deed provide
The spear that pierces the crucified."

And my heart heard me and nailed the tall
Fitz-James fast to his castle wall,
And the spear that pierces the crucified
Sank to its heft to wound his side.

Fitz-James hung from his castle wall;
The cry of his bride from the darkness rang;
And he would fall but he might not fall:
From the nails of my heart he hung.

I laid my hand to my empty breast,
I fingered my aching side apart,
Like one that wheedles a child to rest
Did I call home my heart.

And the hanged one fell to earth by his door
As my heart flew home a silent thing;
It will cage in the clutch of his hand no more,
And save in his clutch it may not sing.

LYRICS

THE GENERATIONS OF THOUGHT

The young tree's reaching root
Spreads from the fallen fruit,
Golden and shaped like day
Before it knew decay.

The infant life, the child
Hopeful and undefiled
Springs from the unity
Love makes of two that die.

And though we guess not how
Thought thrives behind the brow.

The tree and child, who press
Onward to nothingness,
Scatter their seed and mate;
Themselves perpetuate.

And the generations of thought
That know nor root nor sire
Nor seed nor even desire
Prosper and perish not.

THE FIVEFOLD WORLD

Fivefold, this is a world I know
By taste and touch and sight and sound
And scent, whether rose musks may blow
Or apple petals that strew the ground.
Although a strict demesne, designed
For but a single citizen,
Illumined by its sun the mind
Wide are its shores and seas within.

Being planetary in its habit
This world I know, evolved of dust,
Keeps, as all heavenly things that trust
Motion for wings, a constant orbit,
Bearing its populating one
On ordered circuits of its sun.

WHEN FIRST I FARED UPON THE ROAD

When first I fared upon the road
My strengthless shoulders lacked a load;
And leagues beyond by tower and town
It was not care that bore them down.

It was not pain nor ugliness
That sapped my strength, that made me less
Complete or whole in any way;
I gave no strength to such as they.

But of my store each lark and leaf,
Each lovely element was thief;
And soon their various theft had drawn
To them the strength that was my own.

Now having need of it to bear
On older shoulders added care
Where cranes the curving waters cross
I must begin to staunch my loss.

I being broken to the bound
Of sky and water and the ground,
Must gather up my scattered soul
From pool and petal, bough and bole;

And search each lovely thing to find
The parted pieces of my mind,
And go and find my halved heart
In places half the world apart.

THE TRAVELERS

I have come down by many a way
From Dooly to the hills of home,
Though one was best, for if it stray
The meanest road seems good to roam.
And though I have inquired of none
What thoughts with each tall youth abode
As they leaned idly in the sun
And watched me tramp the dusty road,
It was not yesterday time taught,
By keeping me to fields confined,
How there may be escape in thought.
These made a journey in the mind
Until, beyond the hills and me,
They saw, if vaguely and in vain,
The long waves breaking on the sea,
The cities shining on the plain.

ROADS

A pace or two beyond my door
Are highways racing east and west.
I hear their busy traffic roar,
Fleet tourists bound on far behests
And monstrous mastodons of freight
Passing in droves before my gate.
The roads would tow me far away
To cities whose extended pull
They have no choice but to convey;
I name them great and wonderful
And marvels of device and speed,
But all unsuited to my need.

My heart is native to the sky
Where hills that are its only wall
Stand up to judge its boundaries by;
But where from roofs of iron fall
Sheer perpendiculars of steel
On streets that bruise the country heel

My heart's contracted to a stone.
Therefore whatever roads repair
To cities on the plain, my own
Lead upward to the peaks; and there
I feel, pushing my ribs apart,
The wide sky entering my heart.

THE PEARL

I have a house of meager boards
Furnished with such simplicities
A miser or a monk affords.

My larder's space with lack is gaunt;
From my own niggard fields I force
A husky shield to ward off want.

When thirst is bitter in my mouth
I lean to suckle from the earth
Its crystal milk to quench my drouth.

O well I know rich houses stand,
And food is fat and wine is red
On many tables in the land.

But lack has taught me to resign
With grace the thing beyond my reach.
I am content with what is mine.

Somewhere between the much I see
And little may possess must lie
Repletion, and this homily:

Contentment is a pearl of price
The heart may grow between its valves
To cloak the sands of sacrifice.

OF AN OLD BONE I WAS BRED

Of an old bone I was bred,
Flesh enclosed it and a tongue
Made it syllables and said
Words for it when it was young.

Through me is that bone betrayed
Yet again to pain and passion;
Of my present grief is made
Sorrow of the selfsame fashion

It endured a former night
Before he who learned to loathe it
Cast it, pearly sheened and white,
And my own flesh came to clothe it.

LOOKING

I look to the west,
I look to the east,
I look in the eyes
Of man and beast.

In the eyes of man
I think to find
An open gate
To a kindred mind.

But the gate is shut,
But the stare is hard,
But the trap is set,
But the way is barred.

In loneliness
I turn about
From my own kind
Who shut me out,

Thinking: At least
The beasts will brook
Nor harm nor hate
In their long look,

— Only to find
How the dappled mare
Considers her kind
With a dubious stare,

And the circling dog
His kind goes by
With an ominous look
In his side-long eye!

MEN THINK TO SHUN

Men think to shun
Earth's loneliness;
In crowding towns
They feel it less.

Their houses, though,
Have walls which hide
Themselves within,
Their kind outside.

LOATH IS THE LEAF

The tree in the meadow with none of its fellows by
Appears content as any tree in the wood;
Not so the tree of life that will wither and die
In solitude.

The tree in the meadow has room for its boughs to spread,
Its leaves leak each to each the wine of the sun;
But loath is the leaf that shadows the lonely head
Of the bough it hangs upon.

AS I WENT DOWN TO BABYLON

As I went down to Babylon,
That city lying on my way
I tarried at Jerusalem
To take the mid meal of the day;
And going on I chanced to see,
Nailed high on steep Golgotha's hill,
Three shapes as ghastly as could be
And near to death but living still.
The mid-most one they name with scorn
And gave to drink of vinegar,
And wrote: "JESUS OF NAZARETH BORN
KING OF THE JEWS HE HANGETH HERE!"
The pain that wracked the tallest one
He bore with such a princely grace
It seemed somehow a hidden sun
Ringed golden rays around his face.
One look had I and hurried on;
The guards were dicing for his robe
When suddenly there was no sun
And darkness covered up the globe.
Be sure I hastened forth in fear
Nor lagged till day reclaimed the sun
At the ninth hour, serene and clear,
As I went down to Babylon.

O WHERE IS CHARLIE LANGFORD GONE

O where is Charlie Langford gone
That he comes not at set of sun
For friendly visits at my door
As was his wont to do before?
    He heard the Martial bugle blown
And Charlie Langford's gone to war.

Then tell me, how does Charlie fare,
Now that he breathes a foreign air
And talks, with foreign ale for cheer,
With words that I no longer hear?
    He fares as well as any there,
He takes his ease, he has no fear.

What! When the dreadful cannonade
Begins, is Charlie not afraid?
And when the bombs are bursting close,
Is Charlie not afraid of those?
    His teeth would chatter when he prayed
No more than other men's, God knows.

When dreary night displaces day
Are Charlie's weapons laid away?
And, sick and sore in every limb,
Does he lie down to dream of them?
    To dream? Who knows? To sleep? — O aye,
And hell could not awaken him.

THE SPEARMEN THE BOWMEN THE ARCHERS

The spearmen, the bowmen, the archers
Move splendidly back of the brow —
When Steve was one with the marchers
I was alone with the plow.

Lonely among the boulders
And bitter at heart I turned
The earth while the press of shoulders
Moved toward the world that burned.

Still I go forth to the turning
Of earth, the generous loam,
But Steve turned to the burning
World — and won't come home.

ELEGY

My friend being one with the ground
I grow not bitter and sore
At heart, for my heart has found
Cause now to love earth the more

Since he who was fair of face
And dearest of all the race,
Being stricken and lately dead,
On earth has pillowed his head.

TIME CROWNS THE STEM

Now, though the heart be lost
To grief for those who die
Like flowers untouched by frost,
Cut down unseasonably,

While with the waning leaf
The sun grows thin and dim,
The mourner stops his grief
And weeps no more for them

Sown thick in alien sod
Like seed that wait to grow
At the command of God —
Time tempers all his woe

Showing how from the root
Against man's utter need
Time crowns the stem with fruit
Ten-fold above the seed.

WITH LOVE'S INCLEMENT EMBER

Of all the myriad faces
It pleases life to wear
Two I love bear the traces
That pain has printed there.

Their lives are at November.
Of those at springtime yet
For each that I remember
I many more forget,

Though some have loved me truly,
Kissing me if they would,
And I have loved some duly
As truly as I could

With passion deep or shallow,
And fearful of the flames
That grave for hearts to hallow
The heart-remembered names

With love's inclement ember
Whose brand, as under glass
The rose in cold December,
Will neither fade nor pass.

THIS FOOLISH LOVE

This foolish love I bear for you
Did not come by my body's way;
I did not meet and lie with you
On a summer day.

Yet taken by a lesser chance
My heart is prisoner the same;
Your own it is who smiled but once
And spoke my name.

THE DREAM MADE FLESH

As I came by a wooded lane
I thought upon my love again.
I dreamed my love walked in the wood
The sharer of my solitude,
Fairer than the morning sun
That like a lamp of silver shone.

As I came through the woods at morn
Between the holly and the thorn
I dreamed my love walked in the wood
The sharer of my solitude,
Milder than a flower's breath
Dying in a funeral wreath.

As I came through the poplars high
Against the blue, secluded sky
I dreamed my love walked in the wood
The sharer of my solitude,
Gentle as the doe that lies
Imaged in the lion's eyes.

I, as I came a wooded way
All at the closing of the day,
Beheld her figure toward me run
Like spilled quicksilver through the dun
Leaf-layered twilight of the wood.
The sharer of my solitude,
The dream made flesh, beside me lay
Until the dawning of the day.

A RURAL AIR

When the wind goeth round
The rain will fall,
And a dripping sound
Be heard by the wall.
    Love, is that all
When the wind goeth round?

Happen a kitten
Will sleep in the hay,
And the mule be bitten
By flies, and bray.
    What else, Love?
Who can say
When the wind goeth round?

Chance our love
Will falter and die
Like some sick dove
Denied the sky?
    Neither you can say,
Nor I;
For love will alter
And life blow by
As the wind goeth round.

THE MINSTREL

When love was more than gold to find
And time a coin the heart held dear
There dwelt a minstrel in my mind.
My secret thoughts had he divined;
He sang most terribly and clear
If I but turned away my head
To look with love upon a face:
"The lovers of old time are dead;
The grave is all their trysting place."

When youth was burning like a star
In interstellar spaces cold —
Such distances apart they are
Who think they never can be old —
The minstrel touched his grim guitar
And sang: "Behold upon the street
The halt, the old amid the throng,
They too once went on nimble feet;
Once time's unnumbered dead were young."

When years had taken tender care
Of loves unstable as the grass,
And youth to age had fallen heir,
As age may not to youth, alas,
Close by the country of despair
I heard the clarion minstrel sing,
His syllables unclouded, clear:
"Still waspish thought spares not its sting —
When I sing not you cannot hear!"

BY THE WALLS OF JEZREEL

Queen Jezebel, in Syria slain
And given to the dogs to eat
Three thousand years ago, again
Solicits from the street.

But like a palsied one she shakes
With inward fear, she knows no rest
For she with every love she takes
Folds Jehu to her breast.

OF THE FLESH CLOTHED

Though cloth contain
The body's flow
In fluctuant grace,
Yet all men know

What rare design
From foot to head
Invigorates
The modest thread.

OUR LADY OF INCONSTANCY

I met her first when she was dressed
In robes that graced her form like smoke,
And all the fields that lay at rest
Under her faring foot awoke.

I met her next in cloths of green
When the sheared fields were reaped to sheaves,
And every wind that blew between
Shook sounds of summer from the leaves.

I saw her last a gleaner bent
To fill her skirts with fruit as dapple
As sun on autumn leaves, and mint
Perfumed her breath, and scent of apples.

NOW THAT SPRING IS HERE

Now that the year's advanced to spring
And leaves grow large and long
Forget each sorry and rueful thing
Hearing the wild bird's song.

The leaf will fall, the bird will fly
And winter close the year,
But O, put all such knowledge by
Now that the spring is here!

[108]

PASTORAL

With ambling gait and friendly nod
Across the field the cattle plod.
With reach from side to side they pass;
Their tongues dart out and snare the grass.
Their hoofbeats make a thudding sound
That sends a tremor through the ground;
And on the April wind I hear
The clanging cowbells ringing clear.

A dozen daisy clumps are spread
Beneath a white cloud overhead,
And there are dozens more of these
About the browsing cattle's knees.
Sweet-scented apple blossoms cling
To the first budded boughs of spring;
And on the April wind I hear
The clanging cowbells ringing clear.

WE COULD WISH THEM A LONGER STAY

Plum, peach, apple and pear
And the service tree on the hill
Unfold blossom and leaf.
From them comes scented air
As the brotherly petals spill.
Their tenure is bright and brief.

We could wish them a longer stay,
We could wish them a charmed bough
On a hill untouched by the flow
Of consuming time; but they

Are lovelier, dearer now
Because they are soon to go,
Plum, peach, apple and pear
And the service blooms whiter than snow.

NOW IN THE HEART

Now in the heart there is
A sound, as if of song;
Strange, muted melodies
I hear all summer long.

When summer's emerald wings
Feathers of silver show
Something there is that sings
Of hills beyond the snow.

NOW TO THE FIELDS

Now to the fields the bronze men rise and go
About the business of the harvesting.
The autumn sun is all the god they know
And labor all the rite of worshiping
That deity of weather. While the sun
Lamps the round dome of their enormous church
They worship, and till harvesting is done
God is no farther than the fields to search.

THE FALLEN FRUIT

The apple the bough let fall
Because of a strong wind's suit
Lies now by the orchard wall
A rotted and shapeless fruit.

And I cannot think it right
That none should mention in song
How the fruit was lovely and bright
When fast to the bough it clung.

SONG FOR A LATE SEASON

Now that the apple trees are bare
Of fruit and leaf and grass is thin
On windy slopes, and autumn air
Is sharp with frost, and soon begin
The early snowfalls, everywhere
The golden corn is gathered in.

Now that the fallen leaf is sere
And asters wither by the door,
And birds that once called high and clear
Are silent and will call no more,
Now at the old age of the year
Men put the golden corn in store.

Above the houses heaped with snow
Each day the sun is far and cold,
And down each reaped and ruined row
The wind makes mourning manifold,
But farmers warm them by the glow
Of corncribs bursting out with gold.

BY OTHER EYES

The shadow of the fodder stack
Lies halfway down the little field,
Kin to the color of the crow,
Transparent dark, unglossy black,
As, symbol of that season's yield,
It did a hundred years ago.

And yet again it will recur;
That compass shadow east or west
Will by some other eyes be found
Wide-based and pointed like a fir
When I have tired, and been at rest
A hundred years beneath the ground.

TURN OF THE YEAR

As New Year comes again,
By time's turn cleft apart,
Vies the laughing heart
With the heart weeping.

The mirth and gleaming tears
Enter the keep of frost
And are forever lost
To winter's keeping.

Now bends the blighted tree
Before a bitter wind,
Yet this is not the end
Nor last of winter;

Not yet, but very soon
Will winter lock its door
And open it no more
To those who enter

By avenues of frost
That kingdom dim with cold
To seek what from their hold
Is perilous and lost.

THE SPEECHLESS KINGDOM

Unto a speechless kingdom I
Have pledged my tongue, I have given my word
To make the centuries-silent sky
As vocal as a bird.

The stone that aeons-long was held
As mute through me has cried aloud
Against its being bound, has spelled
Its boredom to a crowd

Of trees that leaned down low to hear
One with complaint so like their own
— I being to the trees an ear
And tongue to the mute stone.

And I being pledged to fashion speech
For all the speechless joy to find
The wonderful words that each to each
They utter in my mind.

NOCTURNE

At nightfall in the garden something ghostly stirs,
Never the sound of the softly padding cat,
Nor the dog's stealthy tread, nor the whicker of the bat,
But a moving by the hedges as of whisperers
Walking and talking — of what I cannot hear.

Each night I go to feel the pleasant fear
Of these unknown moving to my ken,
Announced by subtle sounds half alien to the ear,
Their rustling of the leaves more ominous than when
Heavy steps are near.

The wait is vain tonight, as it has always been.
I wait and wait, but nothing is so bold
As to come from mystery into the world of men.
News of strangers coming is rumored on the wind,
But the mind believes nothing its sixth true spy has told.

FEATHERS AND FUR

I saw in a house
Abandoned by men
A timid gray mouse
And a speckled wren.

The wren below
Her nest on the stair
Nodded as though
She were mistress there.

And the mouse, for all
He was timid and poor,
Seemed glad he could call
The floor his floor.

The owners were roaming
Or moved away,
Or waiting the coming
Of the judgment day.

How widely scattered
Or why or where
Little mattered
To feathers and fur.

THEREFORE THE MOTE

O brown rabbit,
Forswear the hedge;
The hound, of habit,
Will hunt the edge,

Then pierce and enter
The shield of shade
At the still center
Of that green glade.

About your arbor
Full-circle, sooth,
Will pass the saber
Of his tooth,

But spare your throat
If plain you lie,
Therefore the mote,
Full in death's eye.

THE TRIUMPH

The rain, advancing hill by hill,
Sounds first indefinite and far,
As water heard through distance will.
Till wetness is its signature
The ear might judge the rain to be
A furtive wind among dark leaves
Or the far sounding of the sea,
Or loud-winged swallows in the eaves.
But when the lances of the shower
From battlements of cloud are thrown
With fury, down from heaven's tower
Against submissive earth and stone,
There's little room in which to dream
The rain is other than the rain.
Still, one can make its roaring seem
A music of heroic strain,
Or seine from it a crying bird:
From some wood-haunting throat I heard
A leaf-remote, a linked refrain
Of notes indefinite as these
That whistle in the pouring drain
Drip from the summer trees.

If one by one the vagaries
The mind has imaged from the shower
Flee like frenetic phantasies
Or petals from the rain-plucked flower,
Yet it is worthy to have heard
A larger music in the rain,
A triumph to have made a bird
Sing in the water down the drain.

OBSESSION WITH WIND

I am obsessed with the wind.
Summer and winter through
And day and night and all weather
The wind is in my mind.
When noon is high and blue
And neither frond nor feather
Find windy reason to stir,
Nor the bough's serrated hand
Hanging bereft of will,
I wish that the wind would blur
The water and sweep the land.
I sigh when the wind is still.

I am the wind's worshiper.
I love the sound of the wind:
Though it be never in sight
I name it when first I hear
It soughing and sighing behind
A hill of pines in the night.
In the day I love its strength
Savage and cool in my face;
I love its hand in my hair
Tugging through all my length
As if it would run me a race.
I am the wind's worshiper.

O, I know the wind is more
Than movement of air unseen.
With swift invisible power
It blows to me from the door
In which the angels lean
Hour on eternal hour.

Their flying hands make pause
And flutter and pray; they bless
Me and my murmuring friend
And name us our names and laws
Which we decipher by guess.
I am obsessed with the wind.

WHENCE FARES THE HEART

How long the heart willed in its secret tower
That the unblooming meadow and the wood
Should break all suddenly into a bower
To shelter the innocent! The young doe stood,
In dream, beneath the elm's green-shafted light,
The downy rabbit, the mottled fangless snake,
The pink-foot dove with eyes of anthracite,
Rested in shadows of the dream's wild brake.

And in this dream there hung, as in a bell,
A pendulum already in its stroke
To sound its malediction of farewell.
The heart, on hearing, neither quelled nor broke
Its prison doors to seek the ultimate
Concession to its dream, for these shall come
Unto the earth, inviolate estate
Whence fares the heart, unhindered of their home.

THE GHOSTLY GRAIN

The things I knew when I was young
Stay ever in my mind,
The tenor of the thrush's song,
The rough palm of the wind

Ruffling my hair the wrong way up
As elders used to do,
And in the morning-glory's cup
The sky drowned in the dew.

Where stone and silence brood I hear
The cocks that woke the dawn
One May day of a vanished year;
And seed by dead hands sown

Grow to a field of ghostly rye
No hand may reap nor bind,
And shadow-sheep graze slowly by
In meadows of my mind.

THE GHOSTLY HOST

When silence broods on field and stone
And time steals to a stop
Feeling, like slack flesh from the bone,
The years slough off and drop,

I dream I hear the sound of rain
Upon the lancing corn
Of twenty Mays ago. Again
I hear the sheep, new-shorn,

Cry as they run bald from the shears
Through morning meadows, green
Anew as if the blighting years
Had vanished from between.

Where clear the sun swings like a lamp
To drive the darkness deep
Beneath the spears of light, a ramp
Descends, and downward sweep

The dead once known, a ghostly host,
To crowd my spirit's rooms;
Then silence in a sound is lost,
Time startles and resumes.

THE MOWER

Whenever the mower would go forth to mow —
Not he the Grim Reaper nor that bundle of bones
That carries a scythe — his stroke was measured and slow;
He had an eye before him to ferret the stones
From the clumps of growth that might hide stony stuff.
It was always August, after the crops were done,
And as he cut the growth of hedgerow or bluff
He seemed himself one slowly mowed by the sun.

Cleanly a swath snaked back behind his blade
But he was not one to be taken in,
Duped by appearances: The shine and shade
Of a single season would bring the growth again.
He dreamed sometimes that spring pursued behind
And all but overtook him up the swath
Before he had done; and yet with such a mind
For the matter his hands were steady on the snath.

Sometimes he knew, strangest unlikelihood,
Amidst the dull toil in the sweltry day
A flash of beauty to quicken in his blood
A memory time could not take away.
Such was the wonder he beheld with awe
When through the dew-spray mowing at morning made
A lance of sun came piercing, and he saw
Rainbow on rainbow widening from his blade.

THE LADY OF QUALITY

The lady of quality
That lived in the lane
Was beautiful in pleasure
And beautiful in pain.
She carried her beauty
Through all her years,
Beautiful in laughter
And beautiful in tears.
She carried her beauty
Past being and breath,
Beautiful she was in life
And beautiful in death.

FROM THE DOVECOTE OF DARKNESS

From the dovecote of darkness flies
The twilight soft and gray;
And shapes with ghostly enterprise
Scale the west walls of day

And lay a siege about my sleep
And hold me prisoner
Till morning comes, at night's cone steep
With wash of light to wear,

And all things don their morning mien,
Putting, like faces, on
Their actualities again
In greeting to the sun.

As morning widens in my mind
The gentle ghosts arise,
And are not anywhere to find
Until with gray and silent throat
At elder evening from its cote
The dove of twilight flies.

THE FALL OF FRUIT

What has been lost in the wilderness of the brain
Has faded into that forest as a hunted hare
Will part, and lose himself in a field of grain.
What has been lost, or what was never there,
Seems beautiful, O beautiful beyond belief:
Pure essence of dear things past, shrunk rinds of grief
Fall with a lonesome sound from the tree of the mind
Like fruit in far orchards no one will go to find.

I LOOKED INTO A DEAD MAN'S FIELDS

I looked into a dead man's fields
As I walked out by kettle lane;
The corn hung ripe in husky shields
Shaped to his hands that not again

Might harvest it to heaps so clean
Of waste the winter-hungry birds
Had found none in his field to glean
And mourned his thrift in mickle words.

I looked as deeply as I might
Into his fields but nothing spoken
Nor any language known to sight
Hinted of any contract broken

Or bond betrayed too deep to mend,
Though he that planted should not reap
And, their relationship at end,
His fields lay wrapped in winter sleep

And he in sleep yon side of waking.
The wind arose as I went by
And brown leaves in the hedges quaking
Shook on the wind a brittle sigh

As if they fathomed the surmise,
The icy analogue, revealed
As I went by with living eyes
Looking into a dead man's field.

I MARK NOW HOW THE GRASS

I mark now how the grass
Is gloomed beneath my shadow
As jauntily I pass
Across the greening meadow.

His lease to hide the sky
Is all too short, alas,
Who soon full length must lie
In the shadow of the grass.

IN THE FAR DARK WOODS GO ROVING

Whenever the heart's in trouble
Caught in the snare of the years,
And the sum of tears is double
The amount of youthful tears,

In the far, dark woods go roving
And find there to match your mood
A kindred spirit moving
Where the wild winds blow in the wood.

THE FIVEFOLD BLOOM

Now cherish for an hour
Life's sweet, five-petaled flower,
The fivefold bloom of sense.
When it, in consequence
Of death's ill wind, lies blown
And scattered over stone
And under rock and root
Life many another shoot
Will thrust abroad again.
But once the wind and rain
Have scattered forth the rose
At sultry summer's close,
Though many a new rose tremble
Through many another season
That which has borne time's treason
Time will not reassemble.

AS I LIE DOWN

I give my love to earth, where I
A longer, deeper sleep will take
Than woken from when night is by,
As I lie down to wake.

To earth I give my love, my love;
I give my love to earth to keep
Against the time, with earth above,
When I lie down to sleep.

GOOD-BY

Never the landscape glistens,
Leagued far about with light
Of dawn, but the loath ear listens
For announcements of night.

Never may summer widen
Her fruitful doors from spring
But autumn, the never bidden,
Is first guest entering.

"Good morning! Good morning!" lately
From life's lips I heard;
Now a dark tongue in a dark place
Shapes a dark word.

ON THE PRECIPICE

Night coming down,
This ledge of stone
Midway the peak
We crouch upon.

Our cramped space is
A balcony
That hangs suspended
From the sky.

In utter gloom
Beneath, a pit
Yawns wide, and we
Hang over it.

Leaning our faces
On the air,
Into the empty
Pit we stare.

Then press against
Our wall of stone
As we would push
The mountain down.

A CONVERSATION

I said to my heart:
I am hard beset,
Like a bird I am caught
In fate's foul net.

And my heart said to me:
Yet do I
Seek but to serve thee
Until you die.

Oh, life, I say,
Though I flee in fear
From forces that slay
Is terribly dear.

And my heart said to me:
Yes, and I
Beat right willingly
Until you die.

Yet, heart, if the breath
Be wasted in strife
Till lovely seem death
And hateful life;

Should the grave seem fair
And the race with men
Too bitter to bear,
What then, what then?

And my heart answered me:
Fear not, I
Beat, beat, beat for thee
But till you die!

FROM THE ROAD

What do you see as you travel the lonesome road?
Little enough;
Familiar bird in the bush, familiar toad
As brown as snuff.

What do you see in the darkness lost, in sunlight found
In the heat, in the cold?
Flowers of fire and frost from the selfsame ground
And the little leaves grown old.

What do you learn on the rambling road, in the lane
If little you see?
What men have learned before, and shall learn again
When the grave has me:

To have, to hold the things that I may not keep
For a little while;
To render them up at the ultimate gate of sleep,
Not with tears, with a smile.

ON DREAMING OF ASCENDING TO
PARADISE ON FOOT

Knowing in sleep a pure disbodiment
The essential I rose from its figure prone
Upon night's axis, and like a pilgrim bent
To some far shrine, was on a journey gone.
The way was upward; soon all plains so far
Below me lay the distances my eyes
Beheld were such as measure star from star,
And suddenly I knew I went to paradise.
South on a peak that shouldered at the sun
I met two riders in an ancient car
By such a road my fathers drove upon
When cattle drew the coach of avatar
Descending, and what meant it I could guess,
Having sleep's prescience with which to know:
The Lord this pilgrimage does nowise bless
Except in going each with effort go.
Later the road was path and mine alone
And loneliest beneath the highest peak.
Under that summit surely no foot had gone,
No other wanderer had come to seek
The ultimate pure space beneath the rim
Where he who comes is strangely hesitant
To reach that final kingdom over him,
Being concerned with earth where late he went.
Or so was I; yet I must make an end
Of climbing and I climbed the one step more
Though it were surely easier to descend,
And entered heaven — not by gate nor door.
That country is bounded by a county line,
Imaginary latitude of air,
So one approaching does not know in fine
If he be nearing until he is there.

I stood in paradise, no land of thrones
Nor of streets of gold, nor of harps, nor of jeweled halls,
Alone, unchallenged, in a place of stones —
Suitable setting for such a quiet as falls
On him just entering. With eager eyes
I looked, and saw the place to which I came
Was my own land, albeit paradise,
Still every stone, still every field the same.
Whatever source the dream delved to reveal
Its wit, it were too great to lose in sleep.
I woke and waking broke from slumber's seal
This axiom for my waking mind to keep:
Each what he loves shall with himself exalt,
And paradise preserve it in his trust.
And may such prophecy prove not at fault
When come to revelation, as come it must.

SONNETS

NOW AUTUMN PASSES

Now autumn passes, and its spell of gold
Fades in the hedgerows from the waning leaf
That lately hung so burning to behold
It seared the eyeballs like the flame of grief.
The amber acorns rattle from the oak
And apples redder than the fires of Troy
Flaring like flambeaux through October's smoke
Beckon alike to thieving bird and boy.

Planter and poacher parcel autumn's yield;
Berry and nut bulge from the squirrel's pocket;
The yellow pumpkins lying in the field
Bright as day's eyeball in its rounded socket
And corn as gold as any minted pelf
The country Caesar renders to himself.

THE COUNTRY HOUSEWIFE TELLS A ROSARY

The country housewife tells a rosary
Of browning beans and crimson peppers hung
From joist and ceiling; in her pantry she
Has stored for winter treats to tempt the tongue.
And safe in cellar, spilling from the bin,
Are apples stored to mellow in the dark
And bring up tasting sweet and earthy when
The apple tree stands winter-bare and stark.

Her husband's axe rings in the autumn wood
Felling the oaken tree to make a blaze
For winter evenings, as warm and good
Against the flesh as sun in summer days.
And comforted and warm these two shall lie
While northers whistle and the drifts pile high.

THE VOYAGERS

The million-sailed Magellans from the trees
That thrid their rusty canvases and lift
On every wind to try the little seas
Of pool and brook end where old shipwrecks drift.
The water bears the latest to embark
And soon that fragile shallop from the beech
The brooding season launched as summer's ark
Will list and sink, Ararat out of reach.

The winter earth through space goes voyaging,
Snubbing a frozen prow through icy seas
By ghostly headlands from which no birds sing;
Her mariners in snow-spume to their knees
Dreaming about a temperate port of trade
Named May, and crystal cargoes swapped for jade.

COLD IS THE COUNTRY

Cold is the country we inhabit now;
The birds that chittered when the sun was warm
Southward have flocked; wild geese have wedged a prow
Through skies that closed upon their wake in storm.
Now to the touch the cheek of day is chill
And air is iron in frost's foundry cast
That sends the hound's cry ringing from the hill
Where sleeps his quarry, burrowed, frozen fast.

The poor, the beggar faring on the road
In rotted rags shake, agued as of old;
I, cloaked in comfort, coated from the cold
And dry beneath the chaff of heaven snowed
Down from December's sky of slate and stone,
Feel their chill chatter at my marrow-bone.

WHERE IS OUR HOPE WHEN SUMMER
IS THROWN DOWN

Where is our hope when summer is thrown down,
Her seeds and petals hidden in the dark
Utter and chancel channels of the ground,
And silence greets who lately heard the lark?
Stricken so close with hunger that we cry
After such tastes of pleasure on our tongue
Winter a season will to each deny,
Where is our hope of sustenance and song?

Not perished utterly nor hushed for good,
Though we bewail them as a man bereft
Of his last hope; within a sun-warm wood
South the bird sings for others and himself;
Safely the single seed through winter's cold
Husbands its image a million million fold.

VARIATIONS ON AN ANCIENT THEME

I

Love wears abroad whatever face she please;
Look first on this, then that, and which is she?
The moon commands the waters of the sea
And yet the tides that lift the heavy seas
Are not so thrall unto the moon as we
To love who, knowing, know not if love be
A flame or shadow, pain or ecstasy,
Or soul or body, or unrest or ease.

Being in essence spirit infinite
The face whereby love is made manifest
Unto each lover is a mimer's mask;
But whether met by day or in the night
And in whatever guise or body dressed
Who knows her presence her name need not ask.

VARIATIONS ON AN ANCIENT THEME

II

Despite love's guardianship I walk with care
Lest my foot find the snares of circumstance;
I trust love's shield for armor less than air
Against the arrows of time's swift advance.
Love may not come between me and my pain
Nor in a spell my sinews lock at prime,
Nor grief forbid ever to come again,
Nor say to coming death: Some other time.

I must declare that love besteads me nought,
And yet when love is absent from the board
I rise from feasting hungry, yet when caught,
And lacking other cloak, in winter's fury
Such temperate airs do thoughts of love afford
I walk through June in freezing January.

VARIATIONS ON AN ANCIENT THEME

III

The heart has speech the tongue was never meant
To make a vocal language, and the eyes
Can speak love's message and be eloquent
Without a word, put questions, read replies.
The lips when silent by a kiss can tell
More than in speech they ever learned to say,
And hand to hand love early learned to spell
Its various message, whether grave or gay.

Think it not strange, then, if I seek to tell
You of my love first by the faintest touch,
Then write there letters for your eyes to spell
By looking in my own; and then, if such
The need be, let my lips begin to teach
The heart's intent by kiss, and then by speech.

GATHERS AGAIN TO SHINING

I am that creature born to eat the dust
The alchemists of bole and leaf transmute
From solvent soil in which the root is thrust
Into the gold and wonder-shapen fruit.
When windy trumpets signal winter weather,
Impelled by such a need as prompts the squirrel
To hoard the hickory nut, I go and gather
A dusty harvest into bin and barrel.

Yet I am he who feasts upon a star;
I taste the sun when eating of the fruit
Shaped in the image of that globe afar
From whence the leaves brought down their heavenly loot
Of light that once unlocked from apple and grain
Gathers again to shining in my brain.

A GREATER SHINING

Man for his morsel has a dusty bread
Served up for nurture from time's under-table
Where it was stored to feed him by the dead.
This diet of darkness had suborn him sable
Save that his form's wrapped in a shawl of sun
Whose needles plying on the crimson course
The blood conducts about his warp of bone
Web his frail flesh into that fiery source.

When in death's attitude the cells go dark
And earth has back again the flesh that rose
From the primeval posture of repose
To reason and unrest, the sun must mark
Its buried atoms, and command them make
A greater shining for the shadow's sake.

SUMMER AND YOUTH ARE EACH
A LOVELY WEATHER

Summer and youth are each a lovely weather
But heirs of spring, by the decree which fate
Wrote in the will, heir autumn also, whether
Or not they would inherit that estate.
From each the winged month, week, day, hour and minute
Perish like moths that flutter and are gone,
And the Pandora-box of time has in it
Emptiness where its stings and treasures shone.

Not one of all who cannot hope to hold
Title from time to any lasting land
But knows a king's realm for a pittance sold
And changeling coins turned dross within the hand
Before the will is read whereby he heirs
The ultimate country no men claim as theirs.

IF TIME BE TRUSTED

All lovely things have far too short a stay;
The violet must fade before its bloom —
Supposing it a suppliant from the way
It's always bowed — can beg an hour from doom.
And lark and leaf know such a calendar
Their hours of song and shade, too brief in span
To bridge the widening chasm of the year
Fall soon therein, and so are lost to man.

If time be trusted nothing is secure,
Therefore the wise will cultivate the art
Of rooting what in time may not endure
Within the ample greenhouse of the heart,
And capture singers wintertime will find
Silent to carol in cages of the mind.

PUT NOT YOUR TRUST IN
WHAT WILL WEAR NOR SPEED

Put not your trust in what will wear nor speed,
Since not in tower of stone nor turning wheel
Is any alms or answer to our need
Of certain refuge from time's thieves that steal
Our lives with fingers flight nor lock can halt.
Clutch for brief keeping moments of delight;
These, winged for flying, still are less at fault
Than lengthy pleasures past and perished quite.

Seeing the blandishments of man's estate
Are transient in time's immortal mass
He may not judge them straitly by their date,
For joy has never sorrow's lease, alas;
And would he not forego, even in speech,
Death, the sole durable within his reach?

PRODIGAL

I

When summer roses bleed by wall and lane
And busy bees build Babel in the flowers
To my own country I shall turn again
Where only shadows clock the passing hours.
There men who wield the scythe and guide the plow,
Contented if the earth that bore may bed them,
Heed the edict sweat-graven on the brow
And give their lives again to land that bred them.

I shall return from eating dusty bread
To seek the peace the ancient hills were wearing
When all the dreams that harbored in my head
Were of departure and the outward faring;
Shall turn my foot from everywhere, and fall
Into the arms that wait the prodigal.

PRODIGAL

II

Yea, I shall turn again to my own land
When breath is miser-meted, and the low
Voice that spoke in youth and bade me go
Fails in the tongues it had on every hand.
I shall return, I shall go home again
To native hills and valleys, where of these
The brooks ventriloquize, and every breeze
Speaks of familiars of hill and plain.

And there when Fall has vagaried the bee
And wrecked the spider's house and sent the bird
To seek the shelter of a southern tree,
No longer willing to be held or stirred
The leaves of life that stem from heart and brow
May join their brothers flying from the bough.

THE NEIGHBOR

Seeing how near my house he has his dwelling,
No farther away than the first house down the block,
I live in constant fear, for there is no telling
When he will come to my door and enter, nor knock.
Someone I wish to have nearby for calling,
Someone to talk with when I have paused in my labor,
Or should I be ill and alone and the shadows falling,
But he my nearest is no such desirable neighbor.

His fevered face has startled me out of sleep;
He has tainted with his gaze all things I own,
He is cold and a cad; and such is his bold effrontry
I could wish him far from whatever address I keep
I could wish one brought the news he had suddenly gone,
I could wish him a one-way ride to a foreign country.

THREE TIMES ALREADY I HAVE
OUTWITTED DEATH

Three times already I have outwitted death;
He came to me first when I was a tender age
But I tore his hand from my mouth to drink in breath;
And again when winter was whirling in windy rage
He touched my lips with fingers blue as an aster
But could not stop my breath from coming and going;
And again he followed me fast, but I ran faster,
Out of the sea before the tide's inflowing.

Again and again will death prove troublesome;
He in his proximate passing will pluck at me
And I evade his grasp. But the time will come
When he will creep upon me and I not see,
Then he will pluck my life, as a leaf from a tree
Between the wind's keen, cold forefinger and thumb.

I AM THAT ONE A HOUSE WOULD
HOLD IN VAIN

I am that one a house would hold in vain,
Preferring continents cast out of doors
To little islands cartographed by pane,
And feel of earth beneath my feet to floors.
I have had counsel from close corners where
The spinning spiders weave a web of doom
For witless flies that from the boundless air
Win to the prison of a narrow room.

And I am he who entering a gate
Leaves it ajar for going forth again;
I am that homeless one who loves his fate
To be abroad in nighttime or the rain,
Waiting, with wanderer's fever at his joints,
To take the path death's dusty finger points.

EARTHLY EVIDENCE

Since not theology has marked it out,
Nor sages peering through thought's telescope
Defined beyond the shadow of a doubt
Bounds of the country of his fondest hope,
Each traveler must face into the night
With trepidation, bearing in his mind
Only hearsay directions to the bright
Country he trusts his questing foot may find.

Its name is heaven, and he has the need
For time extended past his mortal range
To prove the planting of himself. If seed
Bear in themselves their image clear of change
Safe from their burial, why not he? And hence
He bears this frail and earthly evidence.

THE SOUNDS OF THE HEART

I. THE BLACKSMITH SHOP

There is a blacksmith shop within the breast;
The smithy's hammer on the anvil rings
By day and night with never a pause for rest;
The forced air from his bellows sighs or sings.
Forged at his furnace, rods of glowing red
Support a structure of a strict design;
Into the hopper whence his fires are fed
Pours the long chute that taps the world's wide mine.

No other smith knows such a task as he
Who labors always at his furnace there;
His striking sledge must ever busy be
Solely in restoration and repair.
He may not rest until, when pleasing fate,
His coals blanch out upon a blackened grate.

II. THE DRUMMER

There is a drab musician in the side
Who has one other duty than to sound
Upon his drum the tempo for the stride
Whether the need for haste or halt be found:
When night approaches he is pledged to keep
Watch by the moons of danger at their full
And make a clamor to withhold from sleep
The single sentry posted in the skull.

Whatever sounds more beautiful may abide
In other sources his is lovely sound,
For once his sticks are to the drum denied
The ear in silence absolute is drowned;
And he has heard his last who gasps to hear
The final drumbeat dying in his ear.

III. THE DOOR

There is a door sealed in the body's wall
On which God raps HIS knuckles day and night
And he within, on taking note at all,
Pauses to question if he hears aright
Before he asks HIM in or meets HIM out;
And then, to further lengthen the delay,
Pretends the knock is lost in the wind's rout
Until, hist! listen! has HE gone away?

No. Yet there sounds the unabated knock.
And quiet keeping, playing he is deaf
The one within plans how with bolt and lock
To bar God's entry till it please himself.
And so the siege, and so the wait, until
The sealed door crumbles to its rotted sill.

IV. THEIR CEASING

And I foresee the blacksmith quiet, his hammer
That rang upon the anvil in the breast
Forging the iron of life in noisy clamor
Reverberating in his hand to rest.
And I foresee the drum, the drumsticks broken,
Wrecked in the sounding of a last tattoo
That once in seeming, as a word that's spoken,
Echo has lief the semblance to renew.

And I foresee the door that sounds God's knocking
Forsake its hinges and fall down in dust,
And those two stare across its late unlocking
With nought between them, as at last they must;
And the sole sentry in the close skull sigh
And sleep, not hearing how the echoes die.

THERE WAS A VOICE CRYING
DOWN THE STREET

There was a voice crying down the street
When Babylon the mighty city rose
From the subjected plain about its feet
Close by the waters where Euphrates flows.
The leper at the gate who stood alone
And scratched his sores smiled at the bitter word,
But where the palace like a jewel shone
Belshazzar's heart grew heavy when he heard:

Woe, O ye builders of towered Babylon!
Woe, O ye fashioners of stone and brass
In wonderful designs who think you clever,
Yet do not heed how hungry is the sun,
Nor know the wind, how sharp a tooth it has,
Nor how these two shall eat your dust forever!